CONTENT

DEDICATION

This book is dedicated to the memory of those who have left this world too soon. May their stories live on, reminding us that even in the darkest of times, love and light always find a way to shine through.

It is also dedicated to everyone who has felt the weight of loss, grief, and mental health challenges. You are not alone. Your strength and resilience inspire me, and I hope this book can be a source of comfort and hope.

And to those who have held my hand through my own darkness, thank you for your unwavering support and love. Your belief in me gave me the courage to face my demons and find the light again.

The preface

It is not a story of hope.

This is not a tale of triumph over tragedy. There are some moments of triumph and some moments of defeat, but it's not a story about triumph over adversity. A candid reflection on what can happen in your mind, as you lose so much through loss and grief and mental health issues. It's a tale of the human experience as we know it, the thin line between suffering and hope, and the search for meaning in this tempest of emotions. When I sit down to start this book, I am a young adult just beginning to emerge out of my teenage years. And yet I am left trying to come to terms with the loss of dear ones, processes suicidal ideation that cripples me and desperately searching to find my place in a world which feels both indifferent and overwhelming. It is a tribute to vulnerability, while courageously asking for help when needed, and the maximum capability of humanity to survive and triumph. It's about revealing resilience in the most sinister recesses of our brain and a testament to how hope never dies. I hope this may reach some people who've suffered that journey and at least soothe them temporarily in knowing it's shared, to suffer is human. And for those who have not yet grappled with these challenges, I hope my experience reminds you that there is always light even in the darkest of times, and we are never truly alone.

Introduction

Time of events we go through is like a cycle. The colors had a dull hue, the laughter could have come from a million miles away and the joy that once filled me was lost in the depths of grief. She had cast the entire world into a dim, endless dusk, leaving me to sift through bittersweet golden shadows in hopes of catching a glimpse of something bright. After going through loss, I was lost in grief. Heavy guilt for "what ifs" and the weight of my own mortality placed anchors over me. It was constant war against a flood of anguish; an unending stream filling the back of my mind seeking to break the levees keeping me sane. My inner demon, a gargantuan thing made of the vapor of grief and self doubt, scratched at my insides, hissed that I would be better off dead. Within the constant embrace of my despair, the world was (and still is) suffocating, and everything felt dark and hopeless, not to mention that I could only cling on to a slight whisper of hope alive in the background that perhaps OVER time the pain would subside. However, as I fought to wade through this murky waters, I found a sliver of strength in me. That spark of defiance ignited from the ashes of my despair. As I discovered in the depths of my grief, a small piece of me remained unwilling to succumb to darkness.

In this book, we chronicle that venture. It was an unfiltered expression of the hurt, the confusion, the fear and my frantic attempt to find meaning that illuminated my darkness. It illustrates the resilience of the human spirit, the significance of asking for assistance, and how we can discover hope even in the most unexpected locations.

1. Submerged in Grief

So many things changed (or seemed to, anyway) and the world sort of slipped sideways and I was left hanging on to fragments of what had been. It was a whisper of news, quite unlike the storm within. It was a phone call that broke my world, leaving me isolated on an island of sorrow. The first wave of disbelief was a blurry haze, an asphyxiating shroud with nothing but strange muting sounds muffling incoming stimuli battering my senses. My brain did not want to accept that it was over, the absurdity of someone who had been an integral part of my universe–disappeared. Weeks melded into one another, days gave way to weeks in an ever-slumping procession within the desert of hopelessness. Even getting out of bed seemed like an impossible feat, a Herculean task against the oppressive burden of grief. Everything melted away in the world, colors dulled to obscurity as they were supplanted by an evanescent gray that matched the black hole in her heart. The laughter, once the soundtrack of our days, had faded into a memory, replaced by the weighty silence of an unuttered mourning. Days blurred into an unremitting empty haze. All was silent except for the minutest whir of my own mind. A continuous stream, flood jealousies of "what if" and "why me?". I had no answers, my heart was shattered and my mind spiraled through the labyrinth of questions where I found only suffering. Loss was a tangible thing, tightening my chest until I couldn't breathe. Each breath after that was a battle, an impromptu and tacit reminder of the air filling up to no longer include them. Even the most banal tasks that were once not at all hard to do became gargantuan challenges. Even eating felt like a chore, with the taste of food bland and dead, reflecting my inner emptiness. Life went down, completely unaware of the turmoil that had just occurred within my heart and soul. Others said they were sorry; their condolences were thoughtful, but empty. They said there was healing and moving on, but it didn't seem possible. These rosy platitudes only further demonstrated for me the gulf between their reality and my own. An inescapable cape of loneliness had draped around. My surroundings pulsed with the hum of life, a vast sea where you could hear activity and connection. Yet I was floating, searching for my space in it. Sights of friends and family reminded me of the empty seat. Their smiles were burdened with pity, their laughter a clarion bell to the silence that echoed within me. It felt like a muted voice of shame in the background, something that was telling me I should have somehow stopped this loss. It was a vicious and unforgiving torment knowing away at the corners of my sanity. It was solidified, unmoving, and yet here I was replaying every second of it, dissecting each little interaction wondering if there would be anything left to have missed that could change the way my story unfolded through grief. But there was no script, nothing to rewind what had already taken place. The guilt was an anchor, sending me deeper into the depths of hell. It started an endless loop of self-reproach, stoking the fires of my inner turmoil. The only comfort came from imagining that I was somehow to blame, that by experiencing the same burden of their absence, I was somehow better memorializing the loved one who had died. Yet, even in my darkest pits of misery, there was a light. A recollection, a giggle over dinner, a precious second — confirmation of lost love in the gaps of my being. Those moments of happiness in a garden were as bright lights, leading through the haze of my misery. They were proof of love that never dies; the kind of love rising out from loss, making room for hope and beauty. A very small thing provided the first spark of hope. Walking in the park where I had created many memories with the one who passed away. Walking past a certain bench I knew well, an overwhelming sense of needing to sit down washed over me. A bizarre tug at the heartstrings of a place you once loved but had begun to mourn. Sitting in silence, it was not unbearable. It was a silence I needed, a silence that allowed me to reflect and process my feelings, and to finally start dealing with the anguish inside of me. Sitting on that bench was just an act of acknowledgement, but it became a point of no return in my journey. And it was a little baby step, the beginning of what may be healing but it was enough. It was a realization as if to say, "You're not alone after all, the world isn't so bad when you make your own." A glimmer of beauty and hope, or that spark of faith that I held on to in hopes it would light my way out of the dark. The grief remained with me, a familiar friend. It wasn't a burden I could easily lose, but one I could find ways to lift. It wasn't a smooth road of healing, but it was one I knew I would take. It would be long and difficult, with many dark days as well as some light ones, but at least with every step I took, I knew I was getting closer back up to the surface.

2. The Weight of What Ifs

The burden of "what ifs" hit me like a wave, unyielding and stifling. In the stillness of an empty room where my beloved used to be, there were only a thousand unanswerable questions screaming in my brain. Could I have done more than that? This catastrophic blindside — could somehow, some way I have known it was coming? Did I not see a clue, some slight change in them that would have forewarned me of the unavoidable? It was as if the construct of reality had been torn into threads of time and decimated by the cosmic wind. Those bright, joyful, incredible memories became shadows of their former selves, forever garbled and distorted with some persistent regretful tinge. Every moment, every laugh we shared, every secret we whispered now came under the microscope for clues. The guilt that came with these never-ending questions felt like a heavy parka forcing on my chest. That guilt silently whispered poison in my ear, how unworthy I was, incapable of love and not having the right to exist among those who suffered from the absence of their lost loved ones. Its voice, a persistent whisper in the back of mind, hissed "You weren't enough." "You were supposed to keep them safe, you were meant to save them." I got stuck in this eternal feeling of painful situation after the other, each worse than the last. I replayed the final chat, the final hug, the last meal we shared trying to find a glimmer of premonition, an inkling that might have changed everything. Instead, there was nothing — only the pain of a hollow absence where comfort ought to be. Sleep offered no escape. It instead turned into a battleground where my subconscious was combatting an unrelenting force of what ifs. The nightmares came, real and brutality outlined the cruel creation we see in our waking hours. Night after night, I would awake sweating and panting, that foul taste of hopelessness on my tongue. The silence, which had once been a haven of solace, turned into a torture device. I could hear the floorboards creaking, the wind from outside rustling tree leaves and every sound nearby became a malicious whisper announcing to me of my life void of them. I was a whirlwind of catastrophe, and the world did not care about it, which made this indifference seem like betrayal. I wanted to hear the answers and tell myself that it was not my fault, I couldn't do anything more. But only gentle torment in the form of endless iterations of "what if," each iteration seeming as sinister as a shovel scraping against soft earth: too late, our ....is gone. It was a cycle of mania into desolation, causing me to bind myself in crucible fashion torture that left me hurt and deep in the oceans of self-blame. The "what ifs" were a choir of ghosts, ever repeating the same buzzard's song. They were persistent and they seeped into every part of life, threatening to devour me whole. Yet, there was also a flicker of hope within the darkest hours - an ember of rebellion that could not be snuffed out. Deep inside, a small voice pointed out that "This loss is not who you are, the 'what ifs' do not define you. You are still alive, and you can choose life again." It was a whisper, barely audible above my grief's deafening roar; but it was enough. Just the spark for a glimmer of hope, a single ember that could not be snuffed out. And as I held on to that glimmer, a determination started welling up inside me. I would NOT allow the what ifs in my head take over. I would be fighting for my life, my sanity, and the soul of the one lost. And through my tears, I would do what I always do — find purpose in my suffering and build myself the fortitude to endure, to flourish, to exist. I had survived; I was not going to be shattered. The "what ifs" would always be there; a reminder of my loss, but they wouldn't define me. I would learn how to live with them, see that they were there and just put one foot in front of the other.

3. Silent Desperation

The world had shrunk. This was a box that had become too small for me, an airless box defined by the walls of my mind and the crushing gravity of grief. It was a world in which breathing was an exercise and walking was like climbing a mountain. Like an apparition I drifted the days by, an empty vessel who was filled with nothing but despair. The world lost its colors, leaving an opaque gray dust behind. I was afloat with no end in sight lost at sea, waves crashing down on me making it feel as if the world was swarming around my body. People uttered to me, words echoed inside a great distance in my interior. It was sympathy, and stories of loss, and attempts at consolation. Yet their words were like the noise of a hurricane, drowned out by the sounds of my own hurt. I entered a state of deafness, inability to digest. I was in a mute, barren prison of sorrow from which I could not escape. It was not only the outside world that seemed far away. As if this deep fog had come down on my inner world too. My mind, that used to be an active cauldron of ideas, was now slow and cloudy. When I thought back about it, the joy that had brought a fire to my heart had been snuffed out. All that was left was an empty, dark shell of a human being. Everywhere I went was a reminder of what I had lost. The music that once comforted me now stabbed at my heart in the painful remembrance of longing and unfulfilled desire. People I knew, friends whose sight used to clarify me with all the ironic glamor of a clear winter night sky, now brought oppressive nullity. The horror did not stop, it was an endless and tortuous cycle of pain, replaying in my mind in a never-ending loop the last moments — what ifs that haunted my very soul. Sleeping had always been an escape from the grim truths of life, but it morphed into a warzone. The darkness that engulfed, I would soon learn, was not salvation from the light but an incubator of my nightmares. I would be thrust into the past and experience again the pain of having lost them. Their faces twisted in agony, last glimmering words disappearing. I could feel myself waking up, slick with perspiration, heart pounding against my ribs, chest aching from remembering them. The pain threatened to overwhelm me at times. To imagine moving on without them was absurd, a sick cosmic joke. Why bother? Why bother carrying on when you had lost the only thing that really mattered? Yet, some gene would protest, would murmur and tiptoe through my dark folds— A flicker, a vulnerable spark that couldn't be snuffed out. Survivor instinct, of course—an all-too familiar rudimentary urge to push onward, scrounge for purpose in the emotion that was anything but light. It wasn't easy. The darkness was strong, it lured me in with promises of release, of oblivion. But I said to myself, 'No. I knew giving in to the abyss would be a betrayal of all they had fought for, all they had loved. And how to take hits, and keep going, even when the world is ugly. So I hung on, nurturing that tiny persistent smoldering ember of rebellion. I permitted myself to actually know that it was okay to grieve, grieve the loss of them. But I also knew it was a dangerous path and one in which I shouldn't cross. Finding a way to exist, to live, to honor their memory, find meaning despite such a devastating loss. I went through my days feeling very isolated. I attended my university, my job, acted like everything was fine and normal, but nothing felt real anymore. Everything felt muted and cloudy, in a black and white world without vibrancy or bright colors. Functioning without a link to my feelings, the world around me. I was departing from myself, trapped in a maze of sorrow with no way out. It was a silence that was like a figure — always with me, practically. It was not the silence, but a profound and oppressive stillness that infiltrated my being. It was the silence of words left unspoken, the silence of feelings encountered but never really felt, it was the silence of a world that had forgotten to make music. I wore my grief as if it was a shroud wrapped around my shoulders, choking me with its heavy burden. It followed me, and could not be shaken off. It was part of me — a shadow that followed my every step. I was terrified to talk about it — terrified of giving away just how much I was hurtin'. **Bolded sentence I feared what others would think of me as weak or broken.** For some reason, I feared that people would judge me if I accepted the fact that my loss was too big for me to bear. So I pulled into silence, walled my heart off behind some dark citadel. It was a lonely prison of misery, but also one where I could mourn openly—without shame. It was my safe space to weep as my eyes closed in slumber, the fear of being perceived absent for once, no explanation required. It was armor that did shield me against the world, and also kept me captive. And it turned into a prison, an airless room where I was able to view only the silhouettes of my heartache. I was stuck in this cycle of pity and despair, what a vicious cycle it is to be on, the never-ending loop of what if and could have been. They went away and so, whilst I waited for silence to break sadness into millions of pieces, I learned how to drown in the deepness of heartache. The loss started to sink in and the mean crushing weight of what I had lost began to weigh me down, down into the dark. My descent was slow and insidious, a creeping malaise that seemed to fill every crevice of my being. In that moment I was aware that I couldn't allow myself to remain there, could not let the void consume me. I needed to stand up too, I needed to find a way out of my silence & escape from my prison made out of pain. But how? How do you shake off what feels like part of your very body, a plague so inextricable that to move apart from this memory would perhaps feel as if dismemberment? How do you manage to find a way to say something when silence feels like your only option, the weight of what you have lost is so heavy? For a couple of brief seconds I caught an inkling of hope. An echo of them laughing, a hope that we had together, a tune that sent waves of their existence through my system. They were the shimmers of light in the darkness – small flashes of illumination which provided a feeble balm. But those moments were few and far between. Soon, the darkness would descend upon me again, the silence swallowing me again. And I? I would be left to wrestle with the tide of my loss and the enormous challenge of discovering a way through that maze of grief (mine or theirs, who knew?) to light.

4. The Shadow of Guilt

The guilt was an insatiable undertow, drawing me further and further down into the abyss. It traveled under the snow, warming itself alive like a sedimentation of loserness, getting more muscular by the day until it rose and made my head with wings chant its litany "What if? What if? What if?" I would replay things and examine each piece of the puzzle, searching for a single act—a moment lost—that could have changed everything. More than just the death, it was the carrying on afterwards, of still being alive. How could I live without them? How was I to be able to breathe, eat and laugh while the sound of them leaving resonated in my soul? Those questions hit me like shards of glass straight in the heart, an unquenchable pain of guilt. Everyone tells you that time heals all wounds and in that moment it felt almost cruel. The seconds that went by were a new reminder of their silence, a dull pain in my heart. This was no straight line toward healing, but rather a jagged disordered journey through the labyrinth of loss. Some days I did not get up, as if in mourning but then sometimes the tiniest bit of hope would sparkle before being knocked back by another wave. Those were the darkest pits of my sorrow and that was exactly when the voice of guilt would get louder. It began with the voice of your own criticism: "You could have done more." "You should have been there." And in struggling with those allegations, I questioned my very being. Why was I still here? Why did they have to leave me behind? It was guilt like with a sense of injustice, knowing deep down that I had no right to live without them. It was an ironic cruelty masquerading as love, a curse in everything but name. I could have left this dreadful survivor costume behind, but instead it shrouded me like a heavy cloak and choked my breath of life. However, in between the guilt there were pocket moments of clarity. I would look at myself in the mirror, eyes showing everything I had been through and thought 'Here you are, gorgeous, alive and need to keep going. And yet, in those moments there would be an ever swelling ember of hope, not unlike the spark strong enough to rebel against utter darkness. The truth was I had no choice. Life had thrown the curveball — as only it can, in its full-fledged madness — and I now needed to catch that ball or otherwise traverse the dangerous waters of grief and loss. Not a journey I signed up for but one that I had to deal with, one that I had to live through. It wasn't like I was never going to forget them, or find someone else to take their place. It had been more of a hunt for surviving, for thriving in spite of their missing. Or rather it was the acceptance of a mess of emotions that was flowing through my veins, the fury, mourning, remorse but also bits of happiness. It was about living with the scars, not as a marker of my loss but an acknowledgment of the love we had together. But the guilt was like a shadow that followed me everywhere. It showed itself in the most surprising ways, through mundane everyday life. And fixing a meal, I would envision their go to plates, the scent triggering reminders both pleasant and not. Whenever I walked down the street, it was a face that got recognition, cueing movement and laughter for someone else that would just dip back into something bittersweet regretful. Even the simplest of things whispered with a bittersweet undertone, a haiku reminder of the life that was, and how it would never be again. It was a never ending loop of sadness, remorse and wishful longing. I found a quote by Rumi, the 13th-century Persian poet and mystic: "The wound is where the Light enters you." It appeared paradoxical at the start, a contradiction in terms. But how could such heavy sorrow, evidenced in pain and loss, guilt unbearable on the shoulders — be light? But as I thought about the words, a new light began to dawn. That guilt, that sadness, the pillar of my suffering, had become a medium, a route by which I could gain entry to a higher wisdom; deeper insight into myself and life. And it was through the depths of my pain that I gained the strength to look more deeply into who I am, what scares me and how I want to view the world moving forward with compassion and empathy. This was not a walk in the park and it wasn't an overnight miracle. The guilt was an ever-present shadow, whispering that I could be doing more, saying the right things, and making the right choices every time (a voice which I now had agency over—to hear or to silence). The point was to recognize the hurt, to grow comfortable with it, and then allow it to be the spark from which I grew. Guilt was a reminder of love, and if that's not deep? This burden, as you may refer to it, I still bear but which can evolve into a strength or an impetus for a better knowledge of myself and my surroundings. It was ominous, a reminder that no matter how low into denial and despair one could sink there was always that endless starry sky, the chance for clarity and purpose in the face of grief.

5. A Glimpse of Light

The next few days became a black hole filled with horrible silence and the pressure of uncertainty that pressed down on my chest made each breath feel like climbing mountains. It was as if the world around me had lost its color — like every hue that ever graced my life vanished, leaving behind a gray void more hollow than I felt. Even the smell of loss lingered in the air, a reminder echoing through my life. The shocked, distant feeling had faded away now to be replaced with an ache gnawing somewhere deep in my gut that I wasn't sure would ever leave. A pain that could not be put into words, a constant pounding on the senses, an endless reminder of what my life had now become without them. There were echoing reasons for my decisions charging at me in tandem, a battlefield of decisions raging in the spaces between 'what if' and the cacophony roaring about so many inconsistencies because I am human. This house, in which everyone laughed and happy faces were seen at all times of the day and always had a glowing light outside with friends or family — now felt like some mausoleum with each room appearing to carry its own ghostly silence spelling out what was so brutally lost. I walked around trying to find some kind of normal, a tiny morsel of stability in the chaos that swept through my life. But there was just nothingness, a chasm that swallowed me whole. Nights, and the idea of sleeping at night inside a calming darkness, had become sheer torture; an awful at-home joke on what those soothing elements had once provided. I could no longer afford the luxury of sleep. My heart raced remembering good times followed by sad ones, where only moments before had brought happiness now were filled with the pain of having lost them. The most deafening void, one that consumed every thought of mind. One of those sleepless nights — curled under a blanket in the dark, watching the rain out of the corner of my eye while staring out the window. Every drop seemed to mirror the tears that had become my constant companion, silent reminders of the pain that carved me hollow. And while watching the rain, something odd came across me. It felt like the rain and I were grieving together: he fell, and so did my tears. And in that moment, between the black of failure and red of destruction came a flash of hope, one which seemed too meager to kick on but far too stubborn to extinguish. Maybe it was the bone-deep fatigue that had finally driven me to my knees, or maybe it was the unspoken prayer for peace that I had held in my heart for days. Whatever the answer, something purple in me said there is still a chance. Because there is still something worth fighting for. Just a trembling voice in the storm brewing inside, but it was enough. An ember of fire, a speck of hope in the great nothingness. I grabbed on to that, for dear life, like a drowning child. I decided; making a clear determination to not surrender to the pull of the black hole that almost engulfed me. This was not a decision borne of strength, but out of the need to cling to something — anything at all. I woke up the next morning feeling mildly defiant; like, no, grief you will not destroy my life and define everything. But I also knew the path before me was going to be long and painful and uncertain. This time, however, it was a glimmer of hope that I felt once again – not very strong but hey, at least I believed for the first time since losing my life. The decision to continue living, making sense of my shattered world life was not some bolt from the blue. Taking it one day at a time, fighting against the current of despair (in some places the tide was stronger than in others). Not one made out of some kind of new-found strength, but from a mere need to find a light somewhere, somehow. That was a decision based on knowing I would never be who I was before the loss. I would carry my scars visible and invisible forever, as an eternal testament to the journey I had been through. But that decision was also motivated by a conviction that these wounds could be strength, evidence of my survival, proof I had come through the unimaginable. Their first steps were hesitant, uncertain; apprehensive and crestfallen. Yet, with every step I took came the meta-awareness that my body was able to do this. It was still a cold, dark world; the hurt and agony of my loss still burned deep, but somehow a little sliver of light had found its way through the shadows that suffocated me and showed me somewhere to go -- what seemed to be a way out -- away from this place in which I had not chosen to remain alive. So I started calling for help, turning to friends and family, sharing openly about what I was going through and giving myself the grace of allowing some vulnerability. That ongoing companion of shame and guilt melted away as I experienced a materialization of vulnerability and the awakening to not being alone. My healing journey was not linear, it took so many turns and I fell desperately sometimes. Yet choosing life, opting to search for meaning in the darkest of times had provided me with a cause, with a reason to persevere, with a reason to discover beauty amongst the rubble that had once been my life. I had welcomed the injury, it was part of me, my story; a piece that shaped my path. My spark, the one that had slowly begun to flicker dimly inside me, was getting brighter and brighter. It wasn't a glaring illumination, but it was sufficient to navigate the tunnel of darkness, a beacon of hope in an ocean of sorrow. But I had company because the road that lay ahead would be long and arduous. Choosing to stay alive, to salvage some trace of meaning amongst the ruins, was a sign that the will to live had survived in me; proof that the human heart can endure.

6. The Myth of Time Healing

Some might say time is the best healer. A nice saying, a good intentioned comment to blunt some of the sharper elements of loss. But the reality is, time by itself doesn't cure. It is a passive onlooker, an invisible bystander to the slow and painful emergence of recovery that takes place inside. Time just helps the wounds find a way to fester, scar up, lose some of their rawness but will not clean them out completely. It's not healing, it's not mending for the hollowness and the echoes of "what if". Visualize an injury so deep, it lights your flesh on fire as the rent splits across you. With time, the wounds will stop bleeding, the borders will dry and something like a scab will rise up. But the mark remains. You can't just put your foot down and take what you choose. In this case, time is merely an accelerant for the next step in the process of healing. It is that time you give it space to breathe and heal. Now is the time for being vulnerable, now is the time for tenderness and recognising that healing takes place over a long time rather than all at once. Grief is a wound and it needs to be cared for. It takes focus, practice, and self-the bravery to face complete reality through its window of your raw awkward instant. It's not a problem you can ignore, or push under the rug and hope it goes away with time. An existing being that needs to be met, felt and known. The myth that time heals all wounds allows linear, predictable trajectories of healing to continue. It implies that you just have to wait long enough for the hurt to pass, the memories to fade away, and for you to return back to normal. This is a very dangerous misunderstanding. It creates impossible standards, it fosters guilt from those not able to "move on" fast enough, and it can make people feel less like seeking help when they need to. The situation is much more complicated and subtle than that. Grief is a complicated emotion, one part cyclone of pain, anger, sadness and guilt; and another part ache of desire. It's the rising and falling of that stream, the coming and going of those waves. It washes over like a tidal wave, daring to drag you under. But sometimes there is a hint of hope, sunlight shining through the cloud cover for just a moment providing sweet relief. The myth of time healing all wounds was an albatross around my neck, personally. It was this constant, nagging pressure — a sense that somewhere on the horizon was a deadline for my grief to go away. This is why it felt as if I was trying to race against a made up timeline, evaluating my own journey against an unattainable pace. None of which helped my feeling that I was failing, not "healing" fast enough, something must be wrong with me as I couldn't deal with this like everyone else. And round and round I went, judging myself for doing exactly what I believed time was meant to heal. But the truth is, healing is personal; it is a kaleidoscope of hurt, strength and self-exploration. You learn to live with the scars, to understand what happened, and you prepare to find a way forward. It's about living with the wound but not tearin it away. It is about understanding that pain will never go away but that you can learn to live with it, incorporate into your life. It can be hard to wrap your head around because, in our society, healing is often portrayed as this big magnificent moment where one goes from being lost and broken to emerging into the light. We are foot soldiers that enter the fray, battle after battle — slowly winning our freedom one day at a time — forging clarity within ourselves and making the choice to sit with excruciating conversations. It's that resolve within, showing up for ME over and over again despite the pain. It is the willingness to ask for help when you need it, to be held by those who love you. Healing is learning to exist alongside the pieces of your history, to carry them with you as both "your passengers" and "passengers"; reminders that you are strong, you are resilient, and you know what love feels like. Learning that this wound, while painful, can also lead to the most insightful understanding and growth. To find not only grace within healing, but rather in the workings through pain. That wound will never go away, but it may transform into a reminder of the journey you have survived, an honorable compassion that one day helps light your way towards a better life. It can help remind you that you've experienced the dark side and come out on the other end of it, more alive, more wise, with a deeper connection to self and life. Time, with its gentle touch, helps the wound to heal... to blend into your narrative, a badge of survival and strength that says you can overcome anything, that you can mend and emerge wiser from it all.

7. Finding Grace in Pain

The world whispered a lie. It said things like time heals all wounds, give it a few days and the gash in my chest would slowly stitch itself shut, well as soon I mean as that great big rip was inflicted when they left. But time, as I discovered, was a cruel trick. It didn't heal, it just gave the raw, oozing wound an artificial layer of comfort. It calloused over the jagged edges, masked the gaping wounds with a fragile veneer of scar tissue threatening to break with the lightest caress. I longed for a reality where the hurt didn't always feel like it was bubbling just under my skin, where they weren't this ever-present thing that made it hard to breathe. I longed for a universe in which their faces were not imprinted upon every surface of my brain, a reminder of what I had lost, what I cannot regain. But life – in its sadistic gusto – had other arrangements. Not to remove the suffering, but to learn how to coexist with it. It was about embracing my scars that lay deep inside, not as memories of my brokenness but reminders of my strength. Day by day, I fought a struggle against the roiling tide of sorrow that never let up—and it was a painfully slow thing. I woke, every single day with the weight of my heart like a stone and a stomach twisting with despair. I attempted to shelf it, to make myself continue on, act as if the ground had not broken from under me. The hurt never left, though — a phantom limb that throbbed, just under the surface." The way my eyes glanced towards the empty seat at the dinner table, my fingers reaching for a phone number that no longer answered, and me unable to look at certain pictures without memories flooding back. It was during still moments when the world stood back and with it went all else but their laughter, their whispers on the wind, themselves in the air like a scent hanging before disappearing. Then the guilt would swell: a chill suffocating wave of self-recrimination. I was alive, I was still breathing and they weren't. I searched for the meaning of their absence; I racked my brain over some divine scheme that justified them checking out early. I looked to the heavens, the stars, the trees, and things that happened randomly during day to day life for answers. The answers — if they were there — remained just out of reach. That was when I started understanding that I was working on an unrealistic image. I was trying to patch a broken heart with one thread that perfectly fit. Or I was trying to find peace in a world that cannot be fixed. And it was at that moment of hard truth where I started to finally see the light. That grief, so fresh and excruciating, was not a failing. It wasn't something to be afraid of and hidden away. Somehow it became a part of me, the love I lost persisted as a permanent stain. It was an affirmation of my soul being, of life breathing into me. Rather than attempting to push back against the tide I started learning how to swim with it. And I felt the pain and I acknowledged the void, and I soaked into being this naked powerlessness that had been my life. I began to understand the beauty in the brokenness and the strength in the scars. But it sure wasn't easy, not by a long shot. Some days the waves swallowed me – buried me six feet under. Yet it was a grace-filled affair, like all things can be, with lights shining through the dark. So I learned to relish those, I learned to appreciate small wins, and found beauty in the places I never thought I'd find myself. My own breathing, sunlight on skin, children playing in the park — it all pulled me out of my head and into something more life-affirming. I found the beauty in the outdoors again, the bliss of a silent morning, that magical feeling reading another good book. This is when I started to see that healing wasn't about getting rid of the pain but rather figuring out how to live with it. Not to forget, but remembering with a softer heart. It was holding my losses, but not as a burden, rather lessons. And discovering the courage to keep going, not having to because I got this but choosing to. It was about preserving their spirit by living a life that radiated with their love, their kindness, their resilience. This was not some linear movement, a straight line from A to Z leading us to Oz. This journey wasn't a straight path, it had its own share of roadblocks, potholes and unexpected turns. With every passing step, with each drop of liquid grief, I slowly turned brighter with a little more light and additive warmth to my soul. I started trusting my instinct, I began to depend upon myself, and slowly-but-surely I discovered beauty in the mess. Not healed, not in the way I had wanted to believe. But I had. I had learned to accept the beauty in the brokenness, to savor the scars that told my tale. And within that acceptance there came a quiet peace, a quiet endurance — it was allowing me to be alive again, love again, to laugh again, just take the next step in this journey of life. I realized that true empowerment is not about escaping suffering, but facing it — and learning to accept the powerlessness of being human. What I learned is that true love is not finely florid or fleeting; it is a choice, a vow to live in a manner that honors the memories of those who perish before us, to keep their love tucked under our hearts, to embrace the ugly and the broken, and move forward

wounded but surviving like blossoms on

graves—changed forever yet still capable of

crafting joy out of this beautiful chaos we

call life.

8. The Strength in Vulnerability

Life became small, turning technicolor into black and white. What was once a joyful warming air with laughter and bustling became the heavy blanket of suffocating silence. I had drifted, pulled under the tide of a grief so deep, so overwhelming that it nearly sucked me down into the abyss. I knew that loss came hand in hand with grief, well at least in my heart I did — I just never expected how heavy a force it would be. It was more than a vague throb; it was the raw burn of flame, raw and burning, devouring everything in reach. Each breath was a battle, each moment a reminder of the chasm that had been torn from my middle. No, there was nowhere to escape too, no welcome from the continuous barrage of sorrow. Locked in a prison of my own making, I was bound by the past both again guide and punishment. Late at night, with everyone asleep and the only sound just my breath up they would appear; "what ifs" What if I had gone a different way? What would have happened if I spoke more or perhaps less? What if I had stayed on a little bit longer? And the questions were an unrelenting cyclone of self accusatory doubts. Those questions were shards of glass that stabbed into the tender flesh of my heart. The pieces of my world were strewn around me, jagged and sharp, slowly melted into the dirt where they belonged. I attempted to corral them, put two and two together, but my hands trembled, blurred with tears. The life I lived, the one filled with laughter and hope — all that promised a bright future; it was like entering into faraway memories, such dreams turning to dust. The hardest thing wasn't just the pain — it was being isolated. The silence. I had people who loved me, who wanted to help, but they couldn't understand how hopeless I felt. Their assurance was of little comfort, their efforts to console all but fail. I fell deeper into myself, making walls of silent trumpets that would never get past my heart: a wall that kept others out but one I was imprisoned by—I was held in torture by my own pickle barrel called the bible. Not that I didn't want to be with people, I just could not stand their pity — their attempts at consolation and sympathy were very difficult to endure. And in their reaching hands I saw a kind of life raft that was just out of reach, and I was instead flailing around beneath the waves. I felt like a burden, had discomfort and I didn't want my pain to move on anyone that cared for me. My guilt had proven to be my invisible, never-ending anchor as it pulled me deeper and deeper down into the blackness of despair. I was alive, I was here and my loved ones had disappeared into the harsh arms of death. I was at best a traitor, at worst, a survivor — the pearl that had been born from the grinding pain of an oyster, now devoid of its former self; a war profiteer feasting off the slaughter of others. Every sunrise felt like a reminder that I survived another day, every heartbeat an affirmation that's my still alive and breathing, and each memory of them was a cruel punch in the gut scene. I wasn't sure how much longer I could take it. I didn't know if I wanted to. I didn't know if I could. The very idea of having to go through another day, another minute, another nothingness reminding me of the void which had consumed my life felt insufferable. I was wandering aimlessly in a dark pit of despair with no way out. Like a glitching record skipping the same painful groove, playing every version of the tragedy on repeat in my mind. However, a glimmer of light started to appear in the dark. It was a glimmer, a murmur of optimism, the smallest germination of strength pushing against the hard earth of my loss. Looking back, the silence I craved was not an escape. My pain, my vulnerability was not a weakness it made me strong. I was sick of faking being okay, to hide behind pain behind forced smiles and fake words. And so, I got tired of the world where we were supposed to be strong and stoic and never show weakness by being vulnerable. What I did realize is that the most profound courageous act was to embody my vulnerability and own the pain, fear, hurt. I started to reach out. I started to talk. I started to let people in. When I shared my pain, my struggles, my fears, they absolutely did not make me weak. It made me human. It made me strong. It enabled me to meet other people who walked a similar path, to find comfort in their understanding; which in turn created a support system that buoyed me through the tumultuous waters of grief. Not a destination, but a journey. But it was not as simple as a solution, it was more of a process. Struggling over the past year and half has been a waltz between pain and hope, but it is one I was willing to go through. I had heard that grief doesn't go away; it shifts. It forms a crucial section of our identity, the blueprint of lost love and eroded pain but also rediscovered inner security. It was not actually a weakness. Vulnerability It was the stuff strength is made from, grace born of. To be naked, to be visible, to be audible, and the capacity of being known. It was a displacement of the need to always put forth our best, it was about surrendering the beauty mark of ease and grace and daring to be in all the imperfection, the cracks, the scars narrating our tales of living. It was the dawning that our deepest power lay not in perfection, but in our wounds, brokenness and vulnerability. Vulnerability was the secret sauce for our hearts to set down their armor, to drop the personas we created for survival, and engage with this world fully as ourselves. And this was the bridge that brought us to others, who had heard our stories and were there simply to offer comfort (and perhaps find it in return) via the smoky laughter of a shared human experience. In the weakness of being vulnerable, in letting our guard down, in confessing what needed work, is where we found our power. It was within our rawest, most exposed moments, at the cusp of our greatest fears that we found a way to push through – to heal, grow and LIVE.

9. Turning Pain into Purpose

My entire world tipped, like the axis had shifted leaving me permanently rocked off-balance. The laughter, the joy, the husky transfer of air to the chest – all of it felt sullied, like an invisible dark cast had been placed on every aspect of my life. Like the universe conspired against me, so I could see the colorful splendor of living but be locked in a black-and-white painting of my own grieving. My body, a container of grief, dense, aching load that I bore through life with a silent shriek in my throat. The void was a chasm in my soul that gnawed on the entrails of being. I just could not understand what I was supposed to do or how to even begin moving forward when the world had felt like such an empty, pointless place. The myth that time heals all wounds became a wicked joke. Time didn't soothe; it was only a canvas on which the anger and pain could grow, become familiar with me, never let go of me, remind me that life is ephemeral but death is unceasingly permanent. The wound transcended the physical, a cleft through stone with rusted edges. However, honestly speaking, I was unable to escape from the hurt. The ultimate torture was trying to suppress it, trying to push myself forward, which only exacerbated the pain. As if not acknowledging the wound is to deny my whole self. It was part of my story, a story I couldn't delete no matter how much I wanted to. I began to change the way I viewed things in this unbearable truth. Not as a victim but as a survivor, I swallowed the hurting. It was mine to cherish — not something to fear or hide — a marker of my great love, an acknowledgement of that life lost, and a growth opportunity for me. That process of accepting the wound was not about forgetting; it was about remembering.

Cherishing all the happy times, the fun, the love, and lessons they brought into your life. It was about enabling their legacy by embodying a life of purpose, transforming that hurt into a source of motivation to survive and as impetus for change; to be the difference we want to see in the world. However, healing was not a straight line. It was a crooked trail based on broken moments, experienced sorrow and more than the saying at the back of my head what ifs. Some days were hard, to the point where I felt completely overwhelmed by the enormity of the wound and almost lost to darkness again. However, I grew to understand these moments as waves, and that they would eventually dissipate. I discovered how to treat myself tenderly, let myself experience the painfulness of things, suffer, and ask for help when I needed it. And in these moments of surrender I did find courage, an unexpected abundance. The courage to reach out, to listen and soothe my story with a listening ear. It was during the vulnerability where I found community, belonging, and a reminder that I am not the only one who is suffering. Making meaning out of suffering was not about muting or numbing the scab. It was about channeling the hurt into a form of motivation to live in such a way that honored those held too close as memories and lived in such a way to create impact. It was about meaning in loss, hope in adversity, and the reminder that even during the darkest of days, humankind can be resilient beyond imagination. It was, I understood, a wound that brought endless agony but also offered incredible opportunities for empathy, connection with the suffering of other lives, and inspiration to work for positive change. A reminder that we are to live in the moment, that every day matters, and that it is our duty to use our time wisely. The process of healing and making a purpose out of pain began when I first just accepted the wound. It was not so much ever forgetting or moving on, but recognition that the pain is valid and solidified in a way that has meaning for my life and from there I can go forward without it weighing me down. My story is one of discovery, strength and hope where it hides in plain sight. Coping and moving on isn't just the line of humdrum cliches we told ourselves — it consists of heartbreak, uncertainty, and moments that make you question everything deep in your bones. Yet it is also paved with moments of surprising beauty, connection and strength. This is a journey that takes bravery, fragility and an open heart – to let the wound be part of us, part of our tale and part of our way. It is a journey that takes us into greater knowledge of ourselves, into clearer sight of the human condition and more grateful in our experience of life. With each step, I started to celebrate the little wins — the moments of clarity, the times when I could actually laugh (and not cry) that began to peek through the haze of my grief. Those were the moments I realized it was okay to continue; that it is a must to keep living, not for those lost lives but in their honor. What I realized was that even finding purpose in the pain had nothing to do with forgetting, but remembering and holding those memories close, but more about celebrating the lives of all those who had affected mine so intimately over these past years. It was about discovering a different kind of happiness, one that came from perseverance and surviving to tell the tale, one that had been refined in heartbrokenness, and most importantly, it was about honoring life.

Re-casting pain into purpose is not an easy answer. This process is a perpetual cycle of learning, growth and self-discovery that happens throughout our entire lives. It's about experiencing purpose within pain, it's about seeing beauty amid brokenness, it is finding strength in vulnerability. It is a journey of bravery, gentleness with ourselves and seeing the wound as something that belongs to us, part of our story, our life. It is a journey to deeper self-awareness, a deeper awareness of the human condition, and an increased appreciation for the tender gift that is life.

And it is a process I still go through every day. And while the pain may never go away completely, the hope, the strength and the purpose I discovered by transforming my pain into a vehicle for growth have become stars in my sky — constantly shining on me through darkness and light alike to show me that a life lived well is one that is more filled with meaning, love, and resilience.

10. Reaching Out for Help

Everything felt like a stage with a performance I was not ready for. The absence of sound was terrifying too — this whole environment around me felt empty and the silence represented that fact arse-over-tits. I felt lost at sea in my grief, unable to cling to anything firm, or tangible. My life in many ways was like the life lived in slow motion, with every step and word filled with a kind of sadness that never seemed to go away. The world was a blur, vivid colors replaced by muted grays and muted hope. I tried to tell myself that time could fix everything. I held on to that conviction, day by day praying it would become less painful, the shadows would disappear and somehow I would be who I was again. But time, it turns out, is not a Panacea that deodorizes grief. It is a persistent wave that keeps crashing ashore with its complementary and duality of pain and healing. I learned the pain would not just go away. Instead, it transformed and evolved and showed up in different manifestations, ingrained into the fabric of my everyday life. But to this day it was always the little nagging voice whispering into my ear doubts and anxieties. I attempted to distract myself, shove it down a rabbit hole but the loss made sure to come back again and again — always echoing. I fought these inner demons for hours upon hours, struggling to come to terms with if they were even real. My anxiety was the same, deep down inside every day I was in a freefight combatting the darkness as I feared surrendering to it. The idea of me hurting me, the idea leaving my loved ones behind all this alone was too heavy to bear. My isolation took a toll on me, and seemed to bear down on my chest under the burden of its weight. Even the genuinely well-meaning people in my life could not understand the extent of what I was dealing with. They said they were sorry for my loss and other things to comfort me, but their words fell flat; the wall I built was impermeable. An outreach attempt, though sincere, only exacerbated my feeling of separation. I was like an island, completely marooned in a mighty ocean of grief and pain without hope of getting to shore, connecting from the mainland of life. That silence that used to have a soothing effect was no longer my friend. There was no laughter, no echoing of the voices that had once filled my world: those who were such an integral part of it—and their absence only added to this enormous sense of emptiness within. And it was in those intensely lonely times the thought of asking for help began to surface. But to reach out was an admission of defeat, proof that I could not shoulder the burden of the pain alone. This thought terrified me and I hated myself for it. I felt scared of being judged, written off as broken or too delicate to understand. I was terrified that if I asked for help, my grief would somehow be diluted and my pain would seem smaller. This was an internal battle, between my ego and my need for companionship. But I was drowning, in reality. I felt the weight of my grief dragging me under from which I could not swim to the surface. I had been fighting for so long, tired of the hamster wheel that ran inside my head. Deep inside, I knew that this battle would be fortune at best; terrible—trying to do it alone. A friend called me one day as They sensed my hopelessness. they spoke plainly, straight from the heart — no judgments. Quoted: "You do not need to do this all by yourself." It was something so simple and yet it really resonated with me. It was a single carved piece of driftwood cast, I felt, into the swirling tempest that was riding within me; my own Helen Keller moment. At first, I was a bit reluctant to do so, stuck in my pride and fear. However, I later saw it not as a weakness but rather strength to ask for help. It was an act of courage to admit I needed help, and open the door for support. And thus, with shaking hands, I took the first step of healing. I sat and called a person who was not family, who I hoped would hear my pain when none of the people in my life could, who would respond to my fear because none of the people I knew were available to ease that loneliness; I just needed someone so they sounded ideal — a stranger — yet familiar enough. This was a big step, and as much as I readied myself for this move, it came with trepidation but excitement embedded within my heart. However, it was a step I needed to make — a small footstep in the direction of the shores of recovery. It was just a little, dark office but in my mind it became a sanctuary, a safe place where I could finally relax and be seen and be heard. For hours I bared my soul; the pain, the fear, the guilt, and loneliness that became my greatest companions. It was a vulnerability, a surrender to the unknown; it felt like finally placing down the weight I had carried for so long. As I Voiced this and it did shift something within me. I experienced some relief, as if something was lifted off my shoulders. A judgemental-listener, they offered compassion and reassurance. So they didn't tell me what to do but allowed me to process my thoughts and feelings, the grief I had been carrying. Those small talk sessions were a light at the end, an environment where for once I could deal with my demons and hopefully start to heal. I knew it would take a long time to break myself apart, piece by piece, and reassemble my mind the way I wanted it, but every time I went in for a talk there was a tiny sliver of light in the sack of blackness around me again. I also started creating a community of support, connecting with others who experienced loss and understood my pain. Their stories, their lives, and their persistence became my refuge. They helped me remember that I was not in this alone, my guides, my companions. The journey of recovery was not a straightforward path, nor a clear rise. It was a long journey, with many twists and turns along the way. Some days the hurt stung too close to my heart, the shadows loomed large and nearly swallowed me whole. However, I learned to ride the waves of my emotions and embrace the days when the grief was suffocating without allowing it to take over my identity. I aimed to rely more on my support network, allow myself to find the safety I needed when it was available, and trust that I deserved some kindness. Eventually however, I started to find strength in myself again. I discovered that not being strong is not necessarily a bad thing, instead, it can be your strongest armor. It was through my suffering where I was shown the strength of my spirit, the ability to love and be compassionate and thrive even in the darkest times. I started viewing things with new eyes, noticing beauty all around me, soaking in the laughter and life that had felt so far away. I was still wounded, but I was also in the process of healing, expanding and transforming. Grief lasts a lifetime, but we do not need to walk the long road alone. A Moment of Raw Courage In reaching out for help, you are doing something that shows strength, the resilience of humanity. It is a choice to be vulnerable, to take help from someone and let yourself be loved. Healing is a lifelong journey that takes time, compassion and the ability to let yourself be led by the people who love you. This is a path that will take you to places you never dreamed of; within yourself and others, a place where your power bubbles up and the immense beauty of your strength.

11.   Building a New Foundation

The world was a kaleidoscope of broken glass. A shard of life — of shattered life. When the pain was so deep, so consuming that it made breathing feel truly impossible. It was at those times I gripped so tightly onto the lightest beam of hope, just that little spark saying "you are going to be okay" I had always been a dreamer. I dreamed of a colorful life with laughter and love. However, an abrupt and unwelcome departure of a loved one had dropped me into a dark pit. Everything had changed from the colors of the world to a drab, dull gray. Like echoes fading into silence, my dreams were murmurs drowned by grief's deafening roar. And yet among all the wreckage, I knew still something inside could not give in. There was no way I could give into the dark. To pay tribute to the people I had lost, to live a life that reflected their love; the kind of life that once was. Resilience is really about not having the past go away, and learning to live alongside it. It was not about erasing the hurt, but finding a way to bear it like a goddamn warrior. It was a new foundation, a foundation that accepted the imperfections of the previous one but also believed something real and beautiful could grow out of it. And it was like walking through a dark, thick forest of the unknown. I waded awkwardly through the shrubbery, bitch in a maze. Some days, it felt like progression meant just taking things one step at a time — and sometimes that was even too much, having to try not trip over the loose ground. But I was on the move, with a passive aggressive will to escape. I began with little actions that barely appeared to matter. I dragged myself up each morning, even if all I could manage to do was sit by the window and stare mindlessly at everything going on outside. It had taken me a long time back, to start reintroducing minimal joys in my life – a cup of coffee first up in the morning, a walk in the park or talking with a friend. These acts of self-care, while so small in and of themselves, were like little seeds planted around the wasteland that my grief had become. Weren't numbed, but rather allowed a small thread of hope to begin shedding glorious light on that same crack. And I felt me — the change is so little, with time you can feel it. A faint sense of bliss began to arise in the unlikeliest of scenarios;

a short-lived serenity bestowed like a gentle butterfly landing on my shoulder. Such moments were brief but just enough to reassure myself that I was not lost in the dark, there was still beauty in life even with all the misery. It was not an overnight change, or a cure-all miracle for my heart. It was a long, painful rebuilding process. A slow but sure path to discovering a new sense of self. Perhaps the most important step for me was accepting that grief had no deadline. It wasn't a thing you could wait out, and it would just go away. It was not going anywhere, it was a piece of me, a core element in my narrative and I had to figure out how to include it in my life instead of trying to silence or deny it. It meant being aware of what triggers me, the things that bring all that pain flooding back in ways I wish it wouldn't) and memories that can still feel like gaping flesh wounds. It was to give myself permission to cry, sit in the messy emotions bursting at my seams to engulf me fully, without judgment or shame. But it also was searching for the methods to transform that pain into positive action. I started writing — the emotions were flowing onto the paper, too; it was a release, to have those words escape from this body still trying to digest everything. Writing unmasked itself as my form of self-therapy, a means to reach out and connect with myself, to tackle that which I thought was the most complex mystery — my grief. Putting pen to paper gave me a clarity-wielding, fountaining purposeful sensation. It provided a platform for me, an avenue to write my story — and in that process, I found community with others who had walked similar journeys. What I learned was that grief, left raw and unmasked, is universal. There was a unifying aspect to it — the proof of our capacity for love and loss being deeper. By telling my story I was met with a sense of comfort in the fact that we all share something, we are all on the same journey. The path towards resilience involved not making the pain disappear, but learning how to hold the pain with dignity and fortitude. It was about setting new footing, footing that recognised the broken pieces of the old but dared to invite beauty and strength into existence. It was about learning to live with the scars, not reminders of my brokenness but of a life that whipped me in places imperceptible and then picked me up as best it could; testament of strength, the will to survive, to adapt, to emerge stronger. Once I started moving around in this new world, I began to view it with different spectacles. I discovered beauty in the mundane, quick gestures that cheered other people up, the human spirit bouncing back despite obstacles. I viewed the world as a land of boundless opportunity, not one of hellfire and ash. Many mile markers passed by along the journey, at times I felt I had lost my way, that I was all alone and in way over my head. Each time I made a small progression, gained something — meant for myself — I was regaining all that hope back again. Resilience, I discovered, is not invulnerability; it is the ability to rise. It was about learning to make peace with the scars, not reminders of my brokenness but medals of my courage, my resilience, my capacity to survive, to evolve and even blossom. And through that growth, I discovered a new definition of life. And what I discovered was that living without pain is not the goal; it is to feel everything — the full breadth of experience, both light and dark, joy and sorrow. It was rooted in the process of making sense of the struggle, looking for beauty through the cracks and searching for power whilst being vulnerable. It included a long process of embracing change — Change in the form of evolution, acceptance, self-discovery. It was a journey that aligned my spirit with the definition of strength — not the absence of pain, but the capacity to bear it. It taught me that the thing that was behind me did not determine my future. Instead, it reflected who I was and where I would go in its aftermath — to choose whether I would rise above it, heal from it, grow beyond it, live despite it. And as I traversed this road, the memory of the deceased was my light — neither a weight nor hindrance — but an indelible spark illuminating my passage; it made me who I am today through love and would forever be.

12.   The Power of Small Victories

The world felt different. As if the color had been sucked from everything, as if just like in my heart there was only a gray fog. The days went by and I floated through them like a wraith, my own reflection in the bathroom mirror so unfamiliar it would take all my strength to remember I existed. My breath was labored, like the difficulty of getting one foot in front of another. The numbness of loss had turned into a throbbing pain, one that reminded me there was an abyss where Garrett used to be. The "what ifs" rose in a dine around me like the unanswered cries of ghosts that tormented every thought. Why them, not me? What if I had said something else? What if I had done more? The thoughts would loop in my mind, intrusive and dark, twisting and curling like a spider's web around the edges of my consciousness. My littlest of tasks felt large. Every morning, getting out of bed was like a battle against the heavy burden of grief. Everything seemed claustrophobic, the silence screaming that I had lost some important people. Every social interaction was a chore, and every conversation an echo of the laughter we shared, the inside jokes, the eye contacts that now only resided in pieces tucked away in my mind. And that was when I stumbled on an act of kindness — a glimmer through the darkness; something so straightforward. Someone smiled at me, and broke through the icy cold fortress I had surrounded myself in. Their smile, an ephemeral non-event to them, was a life raft for me. It reminded me that there was a world outside of my pain, that connection and compassion still existed. In the following days, I started purposely looking for these little incidents, these insignificant wins. While I was noticing a wonderful sunset, the colors were a brief reminder of something good that still remained. So I did my small part of helping a neighbor up the street with their groceries. Those little things, those small wins became my little lighthouses guiding me through the dark seas. They were like stones dropped into a pond creating ripples in the landscape of my grief. These were proof that I was still alive enough to feel, to care and experience the world through a soft lens. In my case, every little achievement—no matter how small—was a little building block to mend myself. In doing so, it was the initial step in creating a life that paid tribute to the past and opened its arms wide for the future. It was a reassurance that the light, the beauty, the option to be joyful still existed even amongst all this darkness. These little wins laid the groundwork for resilience. These were hardly the grand gestures - a pronouncement of strength that would send shockwaves throughout the earth. They were the secret voices filling me with hope, the soft push that reminded me I was still alive, that I could still feel love, and most importantly had purpose in my agony. I learned strength is not always loud, but rather the ability to pick yourself up when you start to fall, in fact move forward with a broken heart. It is the underwhelming victories that actually show how powerful a human being can be. The healing life trail also was never boxed, it was walking through winding paths with turns you diner expected along the way without armor. Not a pipe race to erase the pain, but rather a long, strange journey of learning how to make sense of living with the scars it created. The biggest victories were actually the smallest ones on this journey. And in the mundane of changing my clothes to clean ones, a message of self-care I had lost while drowned by grief. It was when I actually smiled for the first time in months instead of just forcing a smile. It was the bravery in contacting a friend, revealing my hurt and fragility while understanding that I have someone beside me. These moments were little embers, burning effulgent in the dark, slowly lighting a way forward. And they were living proof that even when the world looked black, very black indeed — there was light inside still burning; a little flicker of resilience that just needed to be turned back on. Small wins have the power to change perspective. If you are wading through grief, it is easy to orbit the huge, impossible. But, when you learn to appreciate little things in life, the vision of looking at this world changes. You begin to see the beauty in your mundane and find joy in your everyday life. Those small wins were the stepping stones through the river of grief. They empowered me to wade into the waters of my own healing, out onto the ever-moving sands of my own emotions. They'd be whispers of hope as though reminding me, I was not alone, of still being able to find meaning in the mess. It is not something that happened overnight, but the deep transformation inside and outside — a slow process of resilience blossoming. It was this concept of knowing that even in the darkest places, there was still a light and that beauty exists, with joy can be found anywhere waiting in the most unlikely of places, within some mundane insignificant thing. Those little wins became my North Star, shining through the haze of grief and showing me a light at the end of this tunnel where I continued to see sunlight streaming past the clouds and warmth from hope touching my skin and purpose in a world that had lost all its meaning for me. Their steps toward resilience were slow dances with grief that gently interwoven the importance of grieving when necessary, but also moving on and finding joy in the unplanned parts of life, meaning from the meaningless. A reminder that even in the aftermath of profound loss, there was still a flicker of life alive and well inside me; the ability to love, the capacity to grow, just waiting for an opportunity to shine bright and flourish. But it was in those small victories, those quiet yet monumental moments of defiance, that I discovered the grace to carry on: keep going, keep living, keep finding purpose amid the

storms of hardship.

13. Redefining Strength

The world went small, imploding around me into that place of nothingness. My body, once full of light and life, became simply a fragile vessel, burdened with an uncomfortably heavy grief that felt like it was destroying me. It was only then that I realized — the world turned and still turned, not giving a damn about my plight. Around me, people walked through their lives, unaware of the void that had formed inside of me. Even though this half-person is all that I had left, even though the spiraling reflection in the mirror would be my only companion for days on end —I still needed

something to cling to, anything at all. Yet

the reality was warped, clouded by the

blanket of despair. It was hard to breathe,

and with every beat of the heart I could hear

a whisper reminding me that things are not

the same anymore. This was the moment,

for me, in my most broken place where I

saw another form of resilient strength. Not

the strength of an armored tank but rather

that of a seed pushing buds upward, cracks

in the pavement, defying all odds in search

of light. It was a survival strength that did

not seek attention, characterized by silence

and grit. I was afraid, fear of nothingness alone was my first instinct, to shut down. To withdraw into that safe place of quiet. To dull the pain after all. To stop breathing, to die, to make yourself a ghost in the world. But deep down underneath my fear, a defiance, a hope — something told me no. I realized that even though the suffering was excruciating, it was not a weakness. This was just pure, immediate grief in response to a true loss. Exhibit in the greater trial of my love for them. Becoming more resilient wasn't about removing the ache or denying it. It was more so about just accepting it, owning it and realizing that is a chapter in my book, that is part of my life. It was realizing that as much as the hurt existed, so did the chance for you to be okay again. It was a painstakingly slow process. Days bled into nights, every moment gasping to breathe. However, I began to find relief in the little things. A real breath, free of that scratch in the throat from all those months where even breathing felt like choking on her own emotions. An instant of happiness triggered from a memory of laughter. Just one day without this strong desire to give up. At this point I started to perceive the world differently. The traditional idea of strength, one that venerated ruggedness as the absence of vulnerability, became hollow and finally a lie. The people I looked up to as strong were not the ones who never fell, but the ones who did and had the guts to get back up again. They weren't strong for holding back their pain, they were strong for overcoming. Not pretending the wounds didn't exist, but a way to heal them. It was about stepping back into the power of vulnerability – not as a weakness. Resilience turned out not to be a one time monumental thing, but an ongoing process. It was a road with literal downturns, crashes and slides but also breakthroughs, progress and delightful surprises. It was a perfect blend of everything, emotions stitched together with the thread of pain, sorrow, anger and also love and giggles. Vulnerability carved the road to resilience Releasing the hold on my need to look strong, releasing the grasp of all those walls I built that protected me from my pain. It was showing up, bumps and all, and exposing my experience in its true rawness. I learned that connection comes from being vulnerable. By sharing my story — by being vulnerable and allowing a space for others to echo their own stories with me — I found community. I was so sick of feeling isolated in my own personal hell that I began to let people see me, more and more every day. What I learned was that vulnerability is strength not weakness. It was the strength to show up as me, to be human, to set down the need for perfection. It was the courage to be visible, audible, tangible. The path to resilience was integrating the self, the light and dark, the beauty and agony. It was remembering that we are not our hurts but rather how fast we can pick up the pieces. It was about rising up against our demons, growing through the pain and becoming stronger from it, more kind-hearted and a better version of ourselves than before. Couldn't forget the pain, but could learn to live with it. To bring it along with me, not as chains and shackles of bondage but a reminder of my courage, my strength, the phoenix that rises from ashes. And a lesson about how to be, the pain I was still feeling that should not have been an enemy that should be fought against but rather its own teacher. During those times when I let myself experience the pain in its entirety, even though it was scary because the last thing I wanted to do was go deeper into the darkness that surrounded me with this heartbreak — is when I found a very deep truth. Strength in adversity, perseverance through challenges does not stem from always being strong. It is born from the bravery to accept our shortcomings, to be vulnerable and then summon up the power of getting back on your feet, stronger than ever before as well as compassionate.

14.   Cultivating SelfLove

And of course, healing is not a straight road. The journey is not a straight line, it has zig zags, threads of deep sorrow interspersed with strands of light, and the endless resolve to take another step. It is in times like these — in fact, especially during challenging situations that self love first starts to bloom. This love is not an emotion that comes and goes; it is a dedication to taking care of yourself, to acknowledging your value even in deep shadows, to knowing on this level that you deserve tenderness, empathy and kindness. Recognizing and accepting the pain is part of self-love. We want to shove away the pain, act like it is not real. However, burying our emotions will only make the scar deeper. We have to allow ourselves to feel the pain, to sit with it, and see that it is multifaceted. It is not about being negative, it is about allowing ourselves the time to process and heal. The most important thing is not to handle our pain so gently. Talk to ourselves the same way we would talk to a good friend. Sometimes we may feel hurt, take a pause and sit with it and offer this little voice: "hey I get it, it's okay to be sensitive". You can be, You know,

I hear that you are in pain at the moment. I am here for you. It's okay to feel this way." That is the absolutely necessary, kind conversation with ourselves. It takes us out of judgment and critical thinking, which opens the door to self-acceptance. We slowly start to realize that we are not our pain. It is the phase that we are at, part of our journey, and speaks of how far we have come and match to what level our resilience grows. Having boundaries is another part of growing self love. It relates to the realization we need in order to distance ourselves from bad vibes and unhealthy situations. We should do OUR best to make ourselves feel safe. Physically and emotionally. It may mean distancing ourselves from draining partnerships, learning to say no to over-commitments, protecting our peace. This does not make you selfish, it is setting a boundary. That recognition that we cannot pour from an empty cup. Before you can give love, we first have to fill ourselves with your own love. This is an act of self-care, a necessary step to creating and nurturing some solid ground into which we can land. Contributing to self-love is also about embracing our talents and recognizing what we achieve. We spend so much time focusing on our imperfections and what we lack, that we fail to appreciate the characteristics which make us unique and talented. We need reminders of our accomplishments—little and big. We have to see how strong we are, the courage we have shown and how far we have come. These wins — no matter how small — are worth celebrating because a huge part of self-esteem is actually positive reinforcement. Reminds us that we are enough, we have value and the right to love. It brings in a level of compassion and support towards ourselves that helps us establish self worth beyond our failures. Loving yourself is an ongoing process. It's not something you reach but have to go through a process for. It takes patience and compassion — we have to allow ourselves to be kind and gracious, even when we are feeling shattered. It is about accepting our flaws, celebrating our strengths and realizing that we deserve love appearing in each form because of being human. Healing from loss and trauma is a bumpy road full of challenges, but those challenges bring the potential for spectacular growth. Self-love is not some luxury; it is a basic need. It is what we can rebuild around, find new purpose, and a resilience that rises above all of our sorrows. This self-love is not simply taking good care of ourselves, but it is being our supporter, our cheerleader and most importantly — our strength. What it means is to choose to love ourselves when everything feels impossible, that we are enough in our own skin. On this complicated road, never forget: You deserve love. You are strong. You are resilient. And that you can heal. Enjoy your journey, be comfortable in your solitude and may the

lamp of self-love light your way.

15.   Discovering New Meanings

It was as if ozone from the loss had permeated the atmosphere. It wasn't simply the lack of their laughter, their warmth, their presence. What had replaced it was far quieter, almost oppressively silent. Everything was black and white, simple as that, the only thing we knew. I was living something akin to a black and white movie, so different from the colorful tapestry of life I had lived before. I always thought of myself as the type who could withstand any storm. However, this loss had rattled me to the bone. The absence of their presence weighed heavy like a ton, the sound of their laughter a phantom limb never straying far away but also an unbearable ache. I would sit for hours watching their empty chair, their favorite mug, their unworn clothes, so clearly evidence of what is no longer here. The "what ifs" gnawed at me. What if I had said more? If only I had more with them? What if I was a nicer person? I kept questioning and these questions were persistent and painful. I started to withdraw, retreating into the dark I already knew. Environment was a surge, way more colorful and audible. Even each interaction reminded of what was missing. I would turn away from phone calls, say 'no' to clicks on invitations and spend my hours mired in the fog of lament. I spent all my days in the same loop, the same soundlessness, the same void. And as I slid further into this shadow, I began to fade. All of the liveliness, all of the love and all of my aspirations were slowly disappearing into miserable nothingness and I was scared. My laughter was a fleeting ghost, too painful to remember the life it belonged to. The world appeared as an alien land, chilly and inhospitable. The same quote that was repeated in my mind, quoted by the poet Rumi: "The wound is the place where the Light enters you." It was a basic saying, but I really captured this in my being. Finally, I started to view my suffering as an entry point, a possibility. That was an uncomfortable truth, to be sure, but it seemed like a glimmer of light in the dark crossroad, a promise in all the hopelessness. I began to cautiously take this new point of view out for a spin. I started to pay attention to the pain, to stay with it, to welcome the dark. I started realizing how powerful I am, the way I could tolerate the hurt. That wound, that gaping hole in my heart, was not something to cover up; not something to be ashamed of. A measure of how great my love had been, the strength of What We Had. When I began healing, I learned that the strength I respected so highly was more than shoving out through the silence of suffering; it was also in knowing how to recognize my pain too and allow myself to submit. It was not about getting rid of the pain but living with it, learning to be comfortable in its company. And, I started to find new meanings — new interpretations of life. That loss had taken a toll on me, it had left its mark on my soul. But it also made me realize how frail life is and what a gift every single moment truly is. It has made me softer-hearted, gentler, aware of the way other people suffer. It was the first thing I thought when I came home after .... committal and collapsed on my couch. The pain has beaten into me the necessity of connection, of extending a hand, to form a community together without even mutually trying. It has made me more compassionate, more understanding, more tolerant of the doubts and paradoxes of the human heart. It has taught me that vulnerability is strength, that opening yourself up to struggle means reaching out for help. The pain it had wrought now rejoiced as my deepest compassion, my will to grow, a reminder of whatever fucking life experience I desired — of remembering how I survived. I had been told that real power was not never being knocked down, but getting up, finding some semblance of meaning even at 3 a.m. But life is funny like that and it was time to reclaim some more meaning where none had existed. Colors blew away from the earth, but were redoubtable to restore it. And so I took baby steps towards the door, and these were replaced with victories, victories of self-care. I began writing again, writing about my pain, releasing the floodgate of feelings that I had bottled up for far too long. It was the one thing I could count on, the one place that offered me any solace in a world that seemed determined to put upheaval in my path. Every single word, every individual sentence, every piece of writing was one more step on my road to recovery – one more step in giving me back my voice. My sense of self. My reason to be here. I build connections and start to figure out how to form a community. I went to grief support, I contacted friends and family, I talked with strangers, told them my story. The road to here has not always been smooth. Some days the ache was unbearable, some days I almost thought the sorrow would swallow me whole. Only, I had grown to welcome the shadows, feeling all of that hurt underneath and allowing vulnerability to give way to power. I had been comforted by the struggles of others, or rather that I was not alone in my struggle. The suffering had also offered me a gift, of seeing through the pain which illuminated a greater appreciation for beauty. I began to appreciate the little things, the simple pleasures, the calm moments of stillness. Instead, I started understanding the way it reveals the resilience of the human spirit, how people can still have hope toward life in times with a blindfolded world. The losing had been so deeply painful, and yet an opening to creating MORE: to becoming MORE. Inspired me to know more of myself and the world, and the spirit of human nature. It has taught me about the power of connection, about vulnerability, and about finding strength in meaning (even when the going gets tough). It was not a journey of removing the pain, it was about learning how to live with it and finding comfort in knowing that its presence is simply part of life. I had learned to embrace the broken, the vulnerable, the painful as beautiful. That scar became a reminder of my strength, a source of empathy and a symbol of the beauty and impermanence of life.

16.   Living as a Testament

I put the weight of survival on me, wrapped in fabric right off the sewing machine. Days started to be defined with dawn — a precarious weight that my being could carry; set against the ever-present insanity of doing this was a silent slaughter. The world vibrated with the ones I had lost, their giggles in the spaces where their actual bodies once were. Their absence was always present, a hollow sound reflecting within me. Life was like a dream, and every step I took, was an act of resistance against the void that loomed to devour me like. Their smiles, their voices, their laughter became my only lifeline to the shore of the living." The void of their absence was a festering, pulsing sore that reminded me, even though there are other great friends and partners in my world, they simply did not occupy the same space. And still, swirling through my grief was a dawning realization — an insistent thought that me living was not just a triumph to myself but rather a vow in their memories. Doubt and regret often tried to silence the echoes of their love. I wrestled with the guilt I created in my head, the never-ending circle of "what ifs" and "should haves." It was like a shadow hanging over everything I did — the question of why they were gone but I was still here. There I was, grappled with survivor's guilt the last few weeks; a walking testament to one of those perfidious twists of fates, an unworthy recipient of serendipity. I had this dream that I would forget their faces, their voices, their very essence. Their memories were rare artifacts, brittle gems, to be bagged and boxed away. Every image an indelible reminder of their lives, each one a physical relic pulling back to happy memories and the laughter they had shared together and the love they had given. The world seemed a little too bright, the colors a little too colorful, the sounds just disturbing sometimes. The noise of life rang in stark contrast to the silence that came with their memory. I withdrew within, where I found comfort in the well-known pain of their absence. I would roll up into a ball in the dark where I could wrap myself with the warmth of their silent being. At those times, I felt almost at home; a bridge back to family and friends and love who were gone — communion with the very soul of their presence. But in the darkness, there was a spark of something, an unfamiliar flame. A soft hint of optimism, a quiet flicker of meaning. I started to understand that existing, despite such immeasurable loss, was not a betrayal but an homage. An act of rebellion that their love could not be erased, that the fire they had lit in my heart could be extinguished only temporarily before roaring back to life. If anything, they remind us that life is fleeting and nothing in this world lasts — most of all us — and so we, best be squeezing every ounce of light from a single drop. I realized I was starting to find comfort in remembering, in sharing stories, in the side conversations, in just remembering. It turned into a ritual, a method of conversing with their spirits: a way of clinging to the love that had been sewn deep within me. I had moved beyond just living. I was thriving. I was relearning to live, to find the pieces here amidst the wreckage, and to use the destruction of it all as fuel for my rebirth and revolution. I held their memory with me like a lantern, more so than light sailing, through the emotional stormy seas of grief and loss. They were love, never in goal ever and spontaneous; somehow their adore was there adding

logical solutions of fortification to it. It was a
strong reminder that love survives, it stays,
it metamorphoses despite the darkest times.
And it is through that love, that ever-present
memory and spirit, that I get my strength to
carry on– to be, to do...to live, to stay alive
(in my heart) –all of it.

17.   Connecting in experiences held common

At the same time, it was like a weight lifted from my chest an atom fraction of the pressure of grief beginning to rise away. It was not an overnight change as if pain disappeared with a flicker of a wand. It was not a huge change, it was the light pull of hope in moments of silence. This was a revelation — a community, a ring of souls who had traveled the valley of loss and grief themselves and come away on the flipping over side, each having earned their scars. For the first time, I was not isolated in my suffering. Not just that some people understood, silencing the others who might not with our mutual understanding of what I'd put them through. It was really the compassionate hearts, the acceptance, living without judgment with eyes that saw past loss and witnessed the strength I was finding. It started with a random meeting. A nervous grin passed across a support group meeting, an unambiguous acknowledgment while the speaker described the perpetual pain of loss. A palpable hush, filled with all that nobody dared say out loud. I remember how, in those first days, the vulnerability seemed heavy on top of me. I was afraid of laying bare my open wounds, the scars that had not healed from loss. As I listened to other people tell their story, their trauma, their vulnerability I discovered strength that I never knew existed. A woman who spoke about her journey with grief described it as a never-ending hurricane that almost devoured her. Something about her words spoke to me, as if I was listening to one side of an argument with only the other half echoing back at me. It would not have been necessary for us to understand in our common tongue the grammar of loss, because the ache was global. And it was then that we were bonded — in the shared experience, in the shared ache, in the shared perseverance. The story she was now telling wasn't a message of hope, but rather a testament to the resilience and capacity to weather the storm and come out on the other side, different sure, but not broken. It served as a reminder that I was not the only one who had to fight this battle, that other people too had fought similar battles and won. The support group became a refuge, a place to release the burden of my suffering. They were a safe space for all parts of me that needed to stop pretending the mask had become unbearable weight, where these things could simply be. It was not about finding a remedy for pain, but about having the company of those who could understand. It was knowing my grief did not have to be a weight I carried by myself, but the invisible thread that weaves us together. They embroidered pain, strength, vulnerability and hope into the fabric of the group. Everyone came with their own story, their scars, and everyone had a different tapestry made of experiences. We told our stories, we held one another up. So we were a quilt of sadness — voices hand sewn with loss, and stitched hearts wearing our second skins like armor. Aside from the support group, I found my tribe online. A digital paradise of sorts where individuals from all backgrounds convened to discuss their grief, loss and mental health issues. But this is where I could engage with others in real-time, to support and be supported. Grief stitched together the conversations in all their ragged honesty, an exposed nerve of collective pain. This was a place to cry, to rant, to heal. A place to be validated, and not feel as though you are alone. The online community became my extended family, my tribe of kindred spirits if you will. More than the words exchanged, it was the knowledge of the experience shared, the silence that hung between them, two survivors mending. It was the understanding that no matter how dark it got, there was light, companionship and familiarity to comfort you through life. It was a place I could practice vulnerability and tell my story without being sentenced to death. It made me think that online people like myself gave some sort of normality amongst the grief. It was in knowing that I was not alone. Despite these, some of the strongest intangible lessons came from the communities — those connections with other people who had walked this path before me. It was the shared experience, the stories told, the discomfort through which we all powered on that helped me mend – to find my own route back to acceptance and peace. Surviving was a comfort, but it did not mean that the pain — or my dead people – had ceased to exist. That all sounded great, but frankly was not about healing for me at the time, it was more trying to live with the pain, how to shoulder loss gracefully and charitably, the meaning in hardship. It was about forgiving myself for my past wounds, not seeing them as a weight, but as gears of strength sufficient enough to turn the wheels of my life that keeps moving forward. It meant that even when things were bleak, caused me tremendous sadness, or held me back so typically despite all of this I could still recognize my place as a part of the race; there would be friends to carry each other through it all. It was about having the reassurance that I didn't have to face these struggles alone, and as a unit, we could meet life head-on with strength and poise. But the peace of living was a blessing, a rare happiness that came from my walking with sorrow. It served as a reminder that though loss was immeasurable, hope existed, connection persisted; there was strength behind vulnerability. It was about searching for purpose in the struggle and the incredible bond of humanity.

18.   The Journey Continues

This was the same park that had provided me a refuge for many years. The sun went down, and it started getting dark — the shadows grew long. Yet this time, the serenity seemed a bitter mockery of my own churning soul. Thoughts furled in my mind, raged like leaves caught in a hurricane — each one screaming that I was empty. Six months after my world had come apart and still the glass of grief broke in my flesh, unhealed. I laid on a tattered seat, metal freezing, glass hot under my skin. I struggled inside, battling between the waves of grief that battered me and threatened to crush me beneath their weight like a sponge diving deeper into the ocean with no hope of swimming back to air, whilst within my heart flickered a flame frail as a long lost ember. Breath was a challenge, heart beating to remind me that I had broken space in my life. This silence rang out, almost as if it were mocking the gaping void that resonated in my very being. However, deep down in the underbelly of my grief was a voice that echoed an alternate story. It told of human determination, how hope could sprout in the bleakest moments. It was a constant reminder of the nights I lay staring at the darkened ceiling, wishing so desperately time travel was possible, I could go back and make everything right again — bring laughter and warmth to the icy void left in their absence. Long gone were the neverending "what if" scenarios feeding behind my eyelids like the white noise of waves crashing into rocks. But the truth was, life is like a river and there is no going back. A river that never turns back, and at times we remain on the banks of a broken heart adrift in their sea of sorrow. I had been paddling on pieces of what was, running my fingers along anything from a part of wreckage, hoping for some direction to quell the inky waters of grief. And, well as the days turned to weeks and weeks to months — I realized this pain was not going away into some great abyss. It was not one of the thoughts that were to be stuffed away in a dusty corner of my mind. That pain nagged me as a reminder of my lost love — the evidence that what I had shared with someone had meant something deep enough to crumble. It was a truth so raw and undeniable that they could no longer dismiss it (and themselves) as people. That healing is the dark and winding road, not a line on graph paper that ever is horizontal or vertical but only seems to spiral inwards as we go it. Some days the pain was just too much to bear, other days I felt like I was in a bottomless pit of despair. Yet there were also days when hope would penetrate the darkness, days when the blanket of grief would peel away — if only for a little while. The littlest things began to soothe me just a bit. An old tune, icecream that shared a night's cloud of laughter, images on paper, smells from happy times gone by. Those snippets of connection were my lifelines, reminding me that still, through the ache, love had found its way into my world and strung a fleck permanently up in the human dollhouse that is left of mine. Gradually, the dim murmurs of hope turned into a choir of strength within. Day by day, I started noticing the power that grew inside of me — A powerful flame, ignited through pain and nurtured through struggle. Just making it through was a victory, and proof of God and what must be this unbreakable spirit in me that cannot ever be extinguished by the dark. Butterflies in the park, One day I was walking through the park and a butterfly sat on my shoulder. For a split second it lingered, wings glimmering as though to soak up the sun; a splotch of color – gray canvas. It was a short-lived instant, merely an action of aesthetics in a world that felt scarce with them. However, in that moment there was peace; a still realization that life- even at its most tenuous- was worth living. It had nothing to do with taking away pain, or moving on from loss. It was to learn how to live alongside the scars, to hold them not as weights that drag me down, but as mementos of love that once graced my existence. It was getting on board with the fact that healing takes time and hard work, it will be uncomfortable, but life changing. Healing is not a destination but a journey. This is not a final state or arrived through high and low, but here we are in the never-ending circle of grief to struggle again. It means realizing that the pain does not reflect any weakness but rather how much we are able to love, and how deep our connections can go. The solace is that survival — with a tone of fearless despair — has its foundation in the confidence to walk into the abyss, to open up to your humanity. It exists in the realization that, no matter how low you may find yourself, there will always be a glimmer of hope; a gentle reminder that life — despite its fragility and shattering moments — is worth living. The journey can be tortuous but it is a worthwhile one, for we find our true selves in the struggle. The sun was dipping down, showering the horizon with a warm dosage of golden magic and for the first time in what felt like months, I was at peace. Healing was not forgetting the pain, it was living with it and finding where we fit in between the cracks. I was now someone different from who I had once been, and yet here I remained, alive, enough, fighting. And that, at its heart, spoke to hope, human endurance.

19.   Hope As A Companion

Hope, at its best, is not a corny, comfort blanket able to wash away all suffering. It is not pretending the dark does not exist, it is bravely acknowledging it exists and then choosing to choose to live in spite of. It's that flickering flame of a candle in a darkened space, the whisper of you are not alone, and even when it gets dark, oh how very dark it can get — but you are still here. Hope was not an epiphany for me but a small, incremental expansion over time. It started small—a drink of water, a breath of fresh air, 1 moment of calm amidst the chaos inside. It was my decision to take what the world can offer even though all it has done is hurt me, a rebellion against the voice that told me to just give up to the void above. As I recall, one of those hopelessly grim mornings, where despair and sorrow had the ability to wrap its heavy coat around me like an unwanted shroud. I could feel myself going down, my body being pulled under by a wave of despair that seemed to drown the sound of my own cries. I acted out of character and picked up a pen and paper. It was pointless – I had no idea what I was putting to paper but the pressure inside me needed releasing. When I started pouring my heart and soul onto paper, something changed... But instead of erupting into joy, I felt some measure of relief wash over me; in that moment all that pain — the feeling that I was just a container for grief and despair — slipped away as realization settled in. This was an act so simple, merely writing, but yet it became a buoy of hope. It was a means, it became almost like this source of connection that despite feeling so completely isolated from the world around me, I could connect with people. And I started to understand that even in our darkest of hours, there are still bright moments, high sparks and glimmers of hope. It was not a straight path that I took; it was a wild, chaotic tango of despair and uncertainty interspersed with occasional hope. I learnt that hope is not a permanent set of mind, it is like a tiny fire that can easily be blown out and needs to be tended. It is something that needs to be nurtured, the active choice to live instead of giving up even when every fiber of your being wants you to give up. It's the contacting, the banging on, of people who 'get it'; of practicing and cherishing beauty.

Hope does not take the pain away - they way you're directly into it. It enables us to make sense of suffering, unearth power at our lowest point and a path ahead when we feel as if the world is physically resting on our shoulders. Hope is a companion, the quiet yet steady figure who whispers in our ear when we feel lost. Then, the dogged belief that the sun will rise again even on the darkest night. The fact that each and every scar is a story of survival, every tear, the testament of our emotions being deep as the ocean and every breath we take — a bonus. That's not the end of a fairy tale; that's where it all really begins. It is a journey that has both shadows and lights, but one we do with hope as our only compass. To those lost, to those who are swallowed whole by the darkness, hope is not a luxury, hope is a necessity. It is the flicker of hope that rekindles your desire to survive, the voice that chafes you not everyone else has simply moved on and need only wait you out but believe collectively with all those who love you that even in such suffering you can experience joy and peace and comfort here within this creation called life. This doesn't mean you forget the pain, it's more about living with it. It takes courage to let the darkness in, to be honest and dirty about the wounds — to then step from that trauma with purpose. Looking back at my own road, I now believe that the best thing ever given to me is not relief from pain but hope through it. Hope, my dear, is the cure against hopelessness — it helps us to heal and a reminder that we can overcome anything and everything, even thrive in darkness.

20. The Gift of Being Able to Bounce Back Resilience.

It really feels like whispering the word devoid – an echo of strength against an echoing void. Something that I wrestle with, something I am trying to put together. I thought resilience was for the strong, the steady, those that could weather any storm and come out unaffected. I never considered myself to be with them. I used to believe, wrongfully, that resilience was a badge of honor, earned after a long walk through something painful. The stories I had read and learned colored my view of what resilience looked like, these tales that promised the dream was made on the underbelly of skill. But resilience is not an honor badge earned for what we have to ixnay through the tragedy. It does not mean pretending as if the pain never happened. And it is something seventy thousand times more difficult than moving; it is collecting your heart after the storm packs a suitcase and leaves. Resilience is less about how to deny your suffering, and more about the kind of acceptance that allows you to embrace it. It's realizing that the cracks in your heart, the breaks in your spirit —

they're not weakness: they're proof of how deeply you feel. Those cracks are the pathways through which light can seep in and brighten up the darkness that nearly overran you. The day when my belove one told me about post-traumatic growth, I felt like someone had just written a title for the invisible transformation I was experiencing. She said trauma could usher in change, it could send sparks through our being so intense they swallow the old and birth the new. My first reaction was to resist this notion. How can something that destroys an entire world drive us into a new one? There are seasons of pain — how is that the springboard to something better? But when I began unpacking the grief and terror, she was correct. Yes, trauma had shaped me, but it also gave me the audacity to face all that terrified me so badly; experience life stripped down to its bones with nothing left hidden or covered. This slow trudge to resilience? Like climbing a mountain — for every step you take upward, you'll take a hundred backward. Some days it feels like the weight of the world is crushing me, some days the tears are at my doorstep and some days I stand face to face with self-doubt. Or the days in which I miss the comfort of numbness, or that silence which had once seemed to be a defected light from haze. But there are bright spots in this darkness. Sometimes I see myself in the mirror and see a sparkle in my eyes and recognize hope, I see the scars — and remember the battles I won (and lost) to earn each one, perceiving them not as imperfections but evidence that I am made of something tougher than flesh. I think it is at those moments where I appreciate its magic; resilience itself. Does that mean overcoming the pain, or does it mean weaving the pain back into my life? It is about acknowledging that the scars I bare are not marks of loss but medals, emblems of my survival and resilience. Resilience is the journey of loving and cherishing who I am today: someone whose body wears scars that tell a tale of survival. It is being aware that the power I carry within me isn't a fixed object but an ever-changing journey, a kaleidoscope of experiences made from fabric sewn together with threads of anguish, optimism and bravery. I am still learning to accept the wounds. I'm still trying to learn how to find grace in all the breaks but they are what make me be me Yet every time I move forward, every moment of acceptance pulls me stronger. I can feel the resilience planting itself, weaving its tendrils into the darkest places of my soul shining light into every crevice I walked tentatively over. When the world is quiet, when I am alone — my thoughts falling away — that calm: never existed before. It is a peace that says we recognize the pain, we accept the darkness, and somehow, despite all of these crazy circumstances prevailing around us, we will rise again. It's the comforting embrace of staying alive, the gentle reminder of persistence that says to you,

"You are not shattered. You are intact. You

are a survivor. You are strong."

Acknowledgments

Writing this book was a deeply personal journey, and I couldn't have done it without the love and support of so many incredible people.

First and foremost, my deepest gratitude goes to my family, who has been a constant source of guidance and understanding throughout my darkest moments. Your unwavering belief and love in me, even when I doubted myself, gave me the strength to keep going.

To my magic, you are the sunshine in my life. Thank you for listening without judgment, offering a shoulder to cry on, and reminding me that I am loved and worthy.

To my friends and colleagues, your unwavering support have been my anchor through every storm. Thank you for always being there for me, even when I pushed you away.

Finally, to the countless others who have shared their stories of loss and resilience, your vulnerability has inspired me and given me the courage to share my own. Your bravery has shown me that we are not alone in our struggles.

This book is dedicated to all of you—the survivors, the healers, and the dreamers. May we continue to find solace, strength, and meaning in the face of adversity.

Appendix

This appendix is intended to provide additional resources for readers who are seeking support or further information about the topics explored in this book.

Mental Health Resources:

National Suicide Prevention Lifeline: 988 /9152987821

 Crisis Text Line: Text HOME to 74174

Grief Support Organizations:

The Grief Recovery Institute:

https://www.griefrecoverymethod.com/

The National Alliance for Grieving Children:

https://www.grieving.org/

The Dougy Center: https://www.dougy.org/

Trauma-Informed Resources:

The National Child Traumatic Stress Network: https://www.nctsn.org/

The Trauma Center at the Justice Resource Institute: https://www.jri.org/our-services/trauma-center/

The National Domestic Violence Hotline: 1-800-799-SAFE (7233) /1091/ 1291

Glossary

Grief: The natural and profound emotional response to loss, often accompanied by feelings of sadness, anger, guilt, and despair.

Trauma: A deeply disturbing or distressing experience that can have long-lasting effects on mental and emotional wellbeing.

Resilience: The ability to bounce back from adversity, adapt to change, and find strength in the face of challenges.

Self-Compassion:Treating oneself with kindness, understanding, and acceptance, especially during times of difficulty.

Sift: To go through especially to sort out what is useful or valuable.

Gargantuan: enormous.

Tacit: understood or implied without being stated.

Cacophony: sounds harsh and jarring because of a lack of harmony.

Arse over tit: vulgar slang–British– so as to fall over in a sudden or dramatic way.

Author's Note

This book Is an inspiration derived from my experience and experiences of several closed ones around me and solely represented to describe "the feelings" only.

To readers of this book at times you feel repetitiveness of certain sentences in different chapter, Please understand the intention in both the places are same but the feelings are different.

For those who wouldn't have enough time to read the whole book Please go through the below "Essay" to get the gist and feelings of the book.

For those who couldn't read or Can't read please go through the attached bar/QR-code and listen and watch the "audio" and "music video" to experience the feelings conveyed through the book.

For those who Finished reading the book, Please feel free to read the essay, Listen to audio and watch the music video.

ESSAY - Survival's Grace

Conflicts, a serious disagreement generally leading to unavoidable arguments. As in as, most of us are aware of the clashes happening in day to day life surrounding us, we tend to forget the conflict we have to go within ourselves.The main reason for such forgetfulness is 'others problems always piques interest providing the drama we longed to see'.Even during such a interesting phase of looking into others, there was mainly one severe clash I have been through all by myself. Yes, small clashes happen from time to time within us like 'a clash between comfort of our body and fashion of our mind while selecting clothes', 'clash between choosing foods that's already a favorite and wanting to try a new flavor' and so on. There is no end within ourselves when it comes to small clashes but the ultimate clash that turns into a conflict within yourself is whether to live or to die, as daunting as it sounds, the one and only experience I could count as a major conflict in my 23 years of life is whether to die or not, rather than whether to live or not.

A traumatic event of losing every loved one around me gradually, from a suicide, from an epidemic ,from an accident.., made me think, what's the use of me surviving alone when no one else around me is alive? What if I plan my death tomorrow? What if I just close my eyes while driving? What if I left myself to drift along the beach? What if... all my plans never work and I survive by that 0.1% chance.... And face societal criticism? All those what if's of survival and demise were more daunting than the decision itself. That's when a fact of realization flashed across my mind " A friend of mine who committed suicide and is peacefully living like a fallen angel*..But what about me? I am still alive suffering from the guilt of not being able to overcome the fact that I could have saved them.." This guilt is what reminded me to live.

The reason is as simple as it is complicated. Would you want to be a fallen angel* or would you rather be a human who doesn't want to be the cause of other humans' guilt.

Time is just too short for any 23 year old to take a huge decision of survival or demise.

But unfortunately most young adults take that decision very rashly because they are afraid that they themselves would conflict theirself, if anymore time was stalled. All such pure souls who once took rash decisions were afraid to face themselves after the failure from the target set by themselves.

All these souls ever required was an assurance from one external conflict, one word of comfort and one person by their side. In a world of 8 Billion people, it isn't difficult to find that one person to be confide to. All these souls ever need to do is "Speak

Up" not for others but for themselves, but if you can't please confide in the one that cries for you and they are that ultimate one person in those 8 Billion people on earth.

Going through traumatic experiences and surviving is a tool for my heart to protect myself and my beloved from all the evil that comes across us. All I ever want to convey is "after a period of crying ,struggling, blaming yourself, failed attempts of suicide and facing harshness of society, comes a period of loving, caring, nurturing and apologies that originally belong to you". Time will never heal the wound, it just creates a grace period to embrace the wound. It upto us, how we utilize our grace period. Be a person who is an example that shows survival is a need [though it hurts], to have that possibility of being your own nebula*.

NOTE :   *Nebula - Character in Marvel Ultimately evolving from villain to Hero.

        *Fallen Angel - The awakening of Demon

LYRICS - - Survival's Grace

(Verse 1)
Conflicts rise like waves on the shore,
Seen the world fight, but inside's a war,
A tug between breathing and letting go,
When love leaves and I'm left alone.

(Pre-Chorus)
"What's the point?" I used to cry,
"Why survive when they're in the sky?"
But then the guilt pulled me back to stay,
And whispered, "Maybe there's another way."

(Chorus)
Oh, fallen angels, gone too soon,
I'll carry your light through the gloom,
Time may never heal these scars,
But I'll make peace with who we are.
Survival's grace is all I hold,
Through every storm, through every cold.

(Verse 2)
What if, what if, the questions ring,
In moments dark, when the shadows cling,
Each thought of leaving fades away,
With the truth that there's more to say.

(Bridge)
In a world of eight billion cries,
All I needed was a hand by my side,
One voice to calm, one heart to feel,
One soul to prove that I'm real.

(Chorus)
Oh, fallen angels, gone too soon,
I'll carry your light through the gloom,
Time may never heal these scars,
But I'll make peace with who we are.
Survival's grace is all I hold,
Through every storm, through every cold.

(Outro)
So here I am, hurt but whole,
Living on with this wounded soul,
Through the grace of life, I'll show,
That survival is the truest glow.

Scan me for the audio

Or Click the link below

https://soundcloud.com/isha-981710187/survivals-grace

Scan me for the lyrical video

Or Click the link below

https://www.youtube.com/watch?v=Svi2zVrRwHk